SUPER POTATO

#8 SUPER POTATO AND THE SOARING TERROR OF THE PTEROSAUR

ARTUR LAPERLA

Graphic Universe™ • Minneapolis

Story and illustrations by Artur Laperla
Translation by Norwyn MacTíre

First American edition published in 2022 by Graphic Universe™

Copyright © 2018 by Artur Laperla and Bang. Ediciones.

Graphic Universe™ is a trademark of Lerner Publishing Group, Inc.

Graphic Universe™
An imprint of Lerner Publishing Group, Inc.
241 First Avenue North
Minneapolis, MN 55401 USA

For reading levels and more information, look up this title at www.lernerbooks.com.

Main body text set in CCWildWords. Typeface provided by Comicraft.

Library of Congress Cataloging-in-Publication Data

Names: Laperla (Artist), author, illustrator. | MacTire, Norwyn, translator.
Title: Super Potato and the soaring terror of the pterosaur : book 8 / story and illustrations by Artur Laperla ; translation by Norwyn MacTíre.
Other titles: Super Patata (Series). English
Description: First American edition. | Minneapolis : Graphic Universe , 2022. | Series: Super Potato ; book 8 | Audience: Ages 7-11 | Summary: Augusta Richly, the world's richest girl, wants a pterosaur, but when her father hires a villainous super-scientist to make it happen, the prehistoric creature escapes and only Super Potato can capture the winged lizard.
Identifiers: LCCN 2021014437 (print) | LCCN 2021014438 (ebook) | ISBN 9781728424583 (library binding) | ISBN 9781728448749 (paperback) | ISBN 9781728444161 (ebook)
Subjects: LCSH: Graphic novels. | CYAC: Graphic novels. | Superheroes—Fiction. | Potatoes—Fiction. | Pterosaurs—Fiction. | Dinosaurs—Fiction. | Humorous stories.
Classification: LCC PZ7.7.L367 St 2022 (print) | LCC PZ7.7.L367 (ebook) | DDC 741.5/973—dc23

LC record available at https://lccn.loc.gov/2021014437
LC ebook record available at https://lccn.loc.gov/2021014438

Manufactured in the United States of America
1-49327-49443-6/28/2021

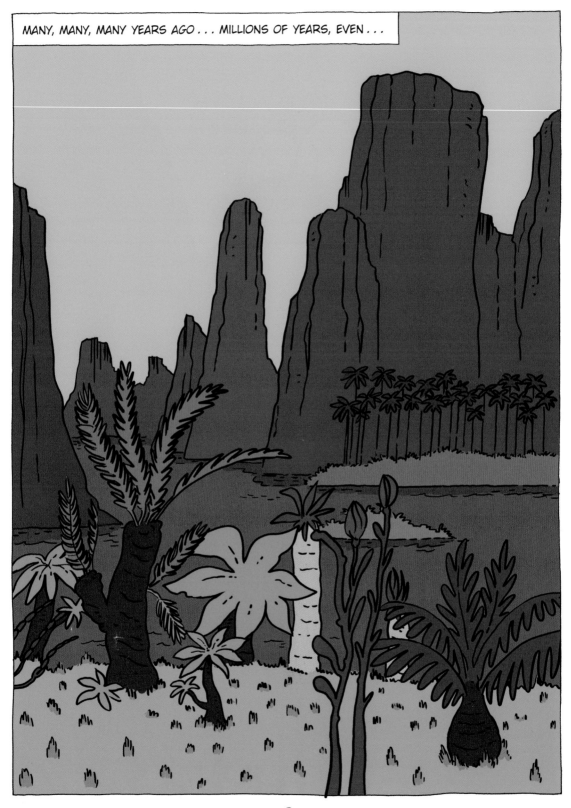

MANY, MANY, MANY YEARS AGO . . . MILLIONS OF YEARS, EVEN . . .

NEAR THE TOP OF A CLIFF...

4

WHICH IS ALSO THE HOME OF HIS DEAR DAUGHTER, AUGUSTA RICHLY . . .

I WANT ONE!!

I WANT ONE!!

I WANT ONE!!

I . . . WANT . . . A . . . PTEROSAUR!!

AAAAAAHH!!

A PTEROSAUR. OF COURSE.

IN RICHLY TOWER, PEOPLE ARE USED TO AUGUSTA'S FITS.

AAAAH!!

I SHALL INFORM MR. BLOCK.

NORRIS, THE TOWER BUTLER, INFORMS MR. BLOCK, THE ASSISTANT OF MR. RICHLY.

THE YOUNG LADY WOULD LIKE A PTEROSAUR.

MR. BLOCK RUNS TO PERSONALLY INFORM MR. RICHLY.

I'LL INFORM HIM PERSONALLY.

MR. RICHLY!

A PTEROSAUR?

AND SO MR. BLOCK TAKES THE ELEVATOR . . .

. . . STRAIGHT DOWN . . .

. . . TO THE DEEPEST PART OF RICHLY TOWER.

STOP WHATEVER YOU'RE UP TO! YOU'VE GOT WORK TO DO!

GREAT. THEN MAKE ONE. YOU PROMISED US THAT YOU CAN FULFILL MISS AUGUSTA'S EVERY WISH.

OH, AND I CAN, BLOCK.

TO START, I'LL NEED A COMPLETE PTEROSAUR SKELETON. FOR INSPIRATION . . .

YOU'LL GET IT. MR. RICHLY HAS A MAGNIFICENT FOSSIL COLLECTION. ANYTHING ELSE?

WELL . . . ANOTHER SODA? SIIIIIP!

THIS ONE'S *FINISHED.*

14

15

THE NEXT DAY, IN THE MORNING . . .

MR. RICHLY HAS HIS BREAKFAST.

SLURRP.

AND IN THE BASEMENT . . .

WHERE'S MY PTEROSAUR!?!

HA HA HA! PATIENCE, LITTLE GIRL!

16

GENTLEMEN . . .
MISS RICHLY . . .
ALLOW ME TO
PRESENT . . .

. . . AN AUTHENTIC PREHISTORIC
PTEROSAUR.

23

MAKE HIM COME BACK!!!

I'M AFRAID THAT WILL BE COMPLICATED, YOUNG LADY.

IT WOULD BE MUCH EASIER TO MAKE ANOTHER PTEROSAUR!

WHAT??

HRRRRM! I WANT . . .

WHAT? WHAT DO YOU WANT?

ANOTHER PTEROSAUR!!

THE PTEROSAUR IS STILL HUNGRY.

CROAAAAK!

AND SOMETIMES YOU DON'T NEED TO REACH THE SEA TO GET SOME FISH.

CROAAK!

WELL, IT'S CLEAR THAT THE TIME HAS (FINALLY!) COME FOR OUR HERO TO ENTER THE STORY. THAT'S SUPER . . . YES, **SUPER** SUPER POTATO. JUST AS HE RECEIVES AN IMPORTANT CALL . . .

CROAAAK!

ATTENTION, SUPER SUPER POTATO! CAN YOU HEAR ME?

I HEAR YOU, GENERAL. WHAT'S THIS ABOUT?

A PTEROSAUR IS CAUSING TERROR ALL OVER THE CITY!!

A PTEROSAUR!

I'LL TAKE CARE OF IT. DON'T WORRY!

IT *DOES* WORRY ME *A LITTLE*...

NO WINGED BUG CAN HANG WITH ME!

A PTEROSAUR IS JUST A GIANT CANARY.

AND HE'S OFF!

QUICK, TURN THE PAGE UPSIDE DOWN!

NOW LET'S TAKE A BREAK FROM SUPER SUPER POTATO AND RETURN TO MALICA, BECAUSE . . .

BECAUSE **WHY?** I'LL TELL YOU WHY.

ALLOW ME TO EXPLAIN.

YOU WERE ACTING IMPATIENT. SO, TO SAVE TIME, I DECIDED TO USE THE SKELETON I ALREADY HAD . . .

I HAVE SIMPLY INSTALLED MOTION NANOSENSORS, ANTIGRAVITATIONAL THRUSTERS, VISION SENSORS, A DUPLICATE MEMORY BASED ON THE BRAIN OF THE FIRST PTEROSAUR, AND A SMALL BUT ESSENTIAL BATTERY, THE WEBSTER LUXOR AC-DC 300-75-1000. QUICK AND EASY!

FOUR MINUTES LATER, A PTEROSAUR ONCE AGAIN TAKES FLIGHT FROM THE ROOF OF RICHLY TOWER . . .

WHERE IS IT GOING WITH SUCH FOCUS?

LET'S REMEMBER MALICIA'S WORDS:

I HAVE SIMPLY INSTALLED MOTION NANOSENSORS, ANTIGRAVITATIONAL THRUSTERS, VISION SENSORS, A DUPLICATE MEMORY BASED ON THE BRAIN OF THE FIRST PTEROSAUR . . .

ITS "DUPLICATE MEMORY" IS THE KEY. THIS PART OF THE ELECTRONIC BRAIN INEVITABLY TENDS TO SEEK OUT THE ORIGINAL.

IN OTHER WORDS: THE ROBOT SKELETON PTEROSAUR HEADS STRAIGHT TOWARD . . .

49

LATER THAT NIGHT, ON THE TV NEWS...

LOOKS LIKE RED IS *IN* THIS SEASON! A MYSTERIOUS RED PTEROSAUR HAS SAVED THE CITY FROM THE THREAT OF AN EQUALLY MYSTERIOUS ROBOTIC PTEROSAUR SKELETON.

WE HAVE WITH US SUPER POTATO, A WITNESS TO THE CLASH.

SUPER SUPER POTATO.

TN9

AND AT RICHLY TOWER...

YES, SUPER SUPER POTATO... WHAT CAN YOU TELL US ABOUT THIS PAIR OF PTEROSAURS?

THEY WERE BIG. VERY BIG.

TN9

HEY!

AAAAAH!!!

HMM... THIS MAY **NOT** BE THE END! WILL SUPER SUPER POTATO DISCOVER THAT THE PTEROSAURS WERE THE LATEST WHIM OF AUGUSTA RICHLY? WILL HE COME FACE-TO-FACE WITH MALICIA THE MALIGNANT ONCE AGAIN? WILL HE END UP THE PET OF THE MOST SPOILED GIRL IN THE WORLD? SO MANY QUESTIONS...

UNFORTUNATELY, WE ONLY HAVE ROOM FOR AN OFFICIAL STATEMENT FROM RICHLY INDUSTRIES:

RICHLY INDUSTRIES, WHICH IS DEFINITELY NOT TO BLAME FOR ANYTHING, HAS DECIDED TO GIVE ONE OF MR. RICHLY'S ISLANDS TO THE HEROIC PTEROSAUR, SO IT CAN LIVE THERE HAPPY AND FREE.

CROAK!!

AND SO WE'VE REACHED THE FINAL PAGE. BUT THIS IS CLEARLY NOT THE END. DON'T MISS SUPER SUPER POTATO'S NEXT ADVENTURE!

For more hilarious tales of Super Potato, check out . . .

**AND TURN THE PAGE FOR A PREVIEW OF
OUR HERO'S NEXT ADVENTURE . . .**

IT TAKES EXACTLY 36 MINUTES AND 16 SECONDS FOR MALICIA TO STOP LAUGHING.

BUT **HOW** TO CAPTURE SUPER POTATO?

THINK, THINK... HMM...

AND ONLY TWO MINUTES LATER...

HAH!

I HAVE AN IDEA!

I HAVE AN IDEA AND I HAVE A **PLAN!**

SMART STRATEGIES FOR

TURNING AN IDEA INTO A PRODUCT OR SERVICE